D0431753

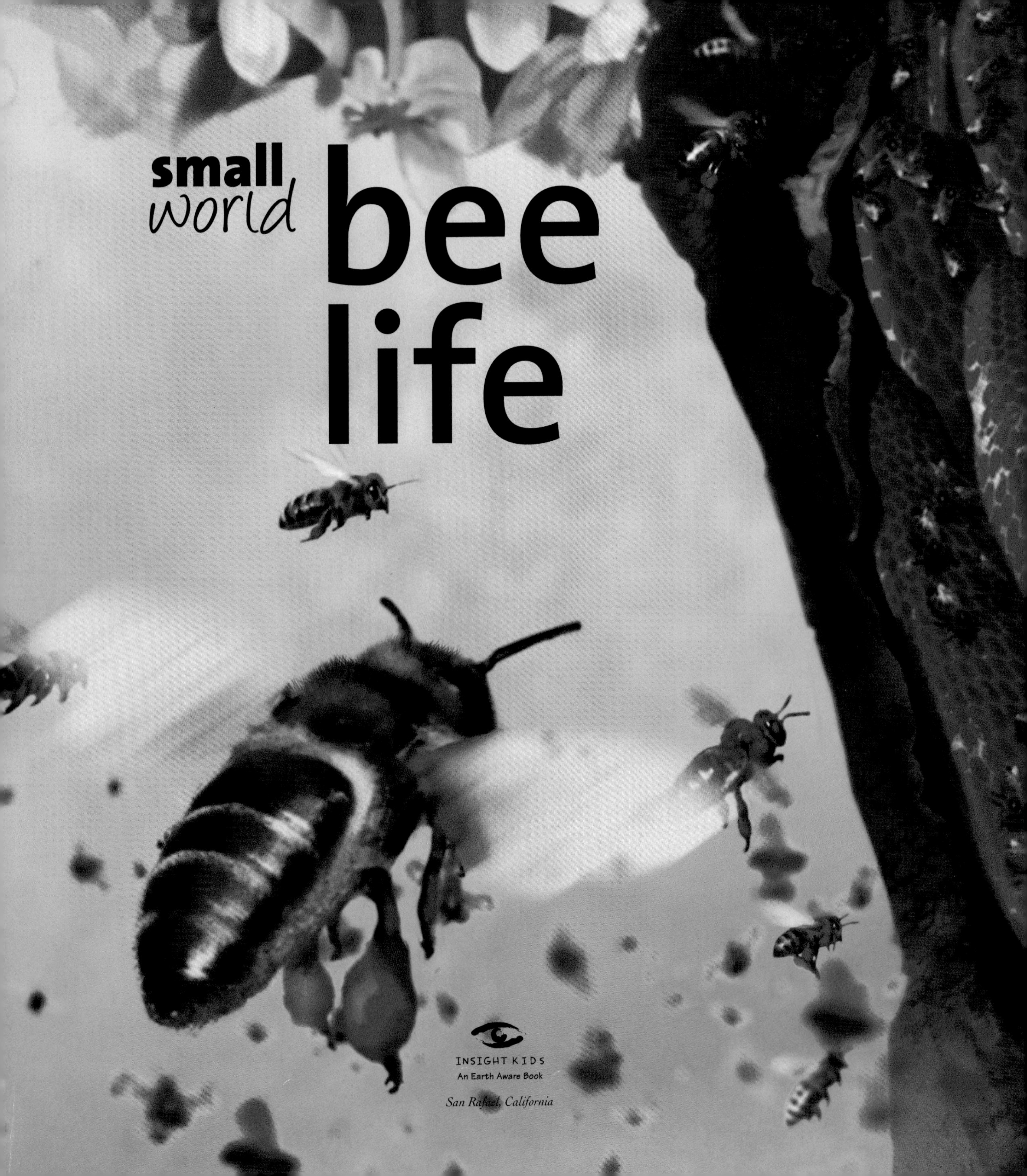

small *world*

bee life

INSIGHT KIDS
An Earth Aware Book

San Rafael, California

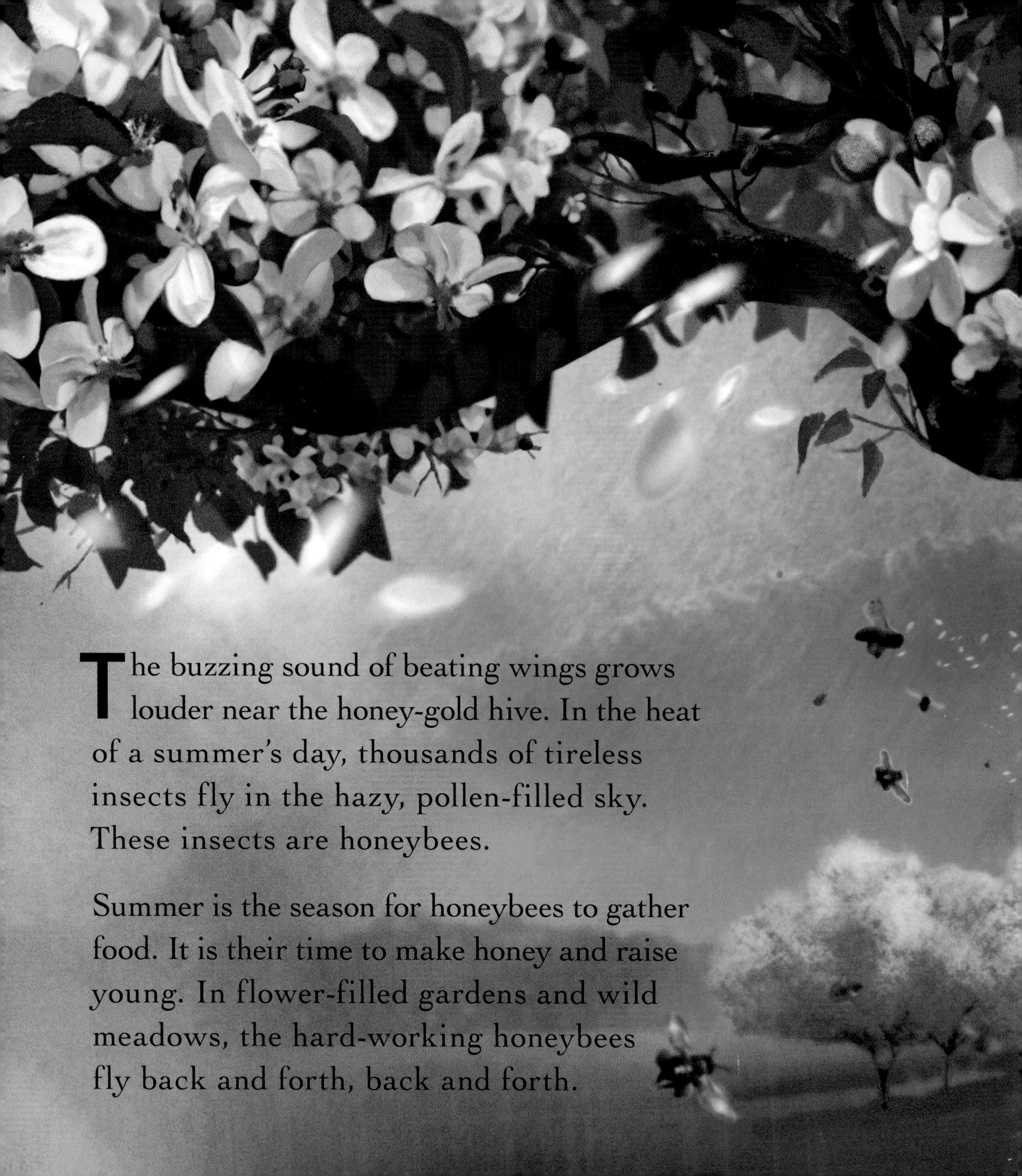

The buzzing sound of beating wings grows louder near the honey-gold hive. In the heat of a summer's day, thousands of tireless insects fly in the hazy, pollen-filled sky. These insects are honeybees.

Summer is the season for honeybees to gather food. It is their time to make honey and raise young. In flower-filled gardens and wild meadows, the hard-working honeybees fly back and forth, back and forth.

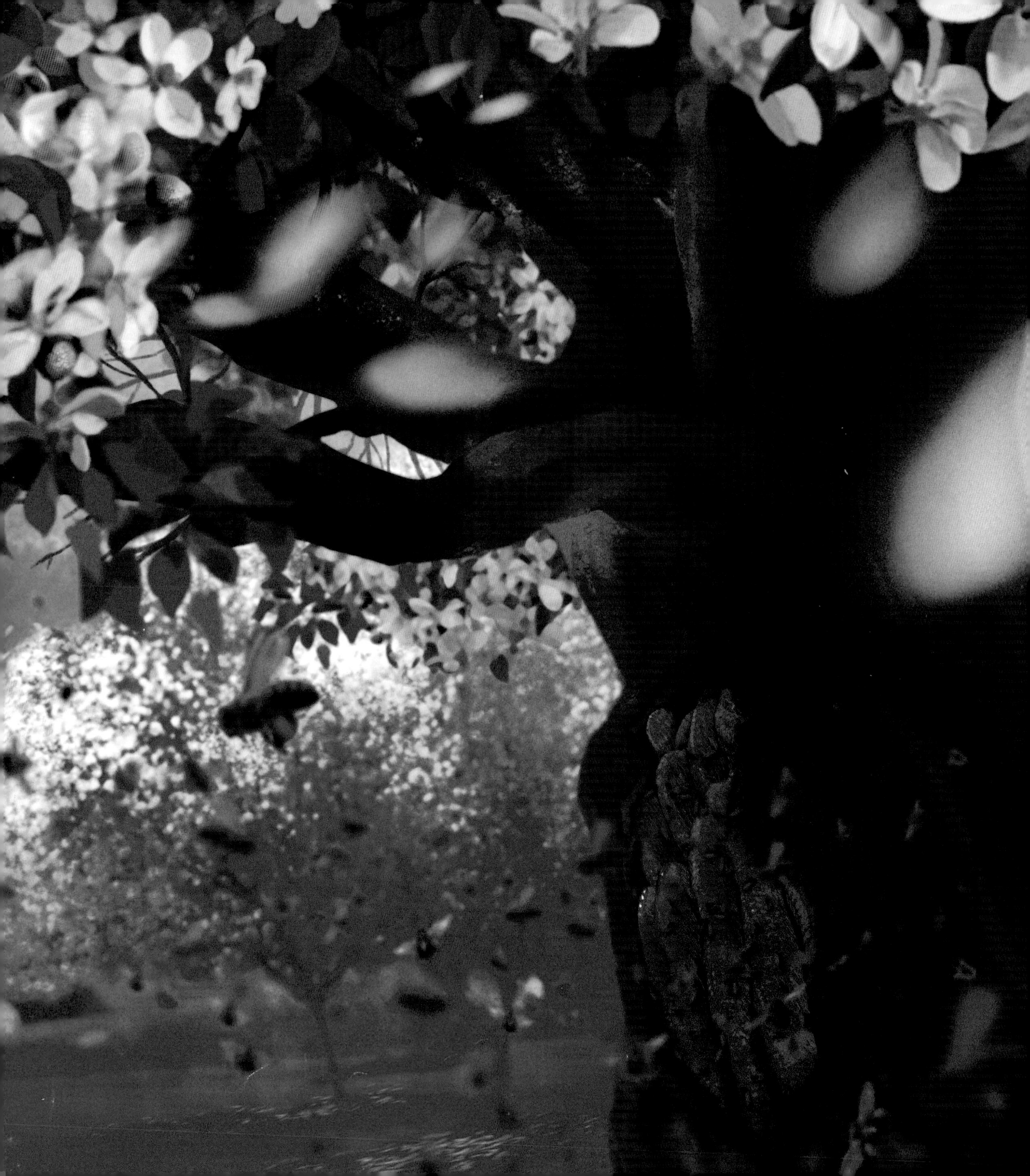

This busy honeybee buzzes from flower to sweet-smelling flower. Her see-through wings look delicate, but they are strong and fast. They allow her to fly forward, backward, and even sideways in her search for food.

The little honeybee settles in the heart of a daisy's unfurling petals. With her long, slender antennae, the little bee smells the sweet flower. As she sips the hidden nectar with her tongue, her hairy body is dusted with pollen as golden as the sunshine.

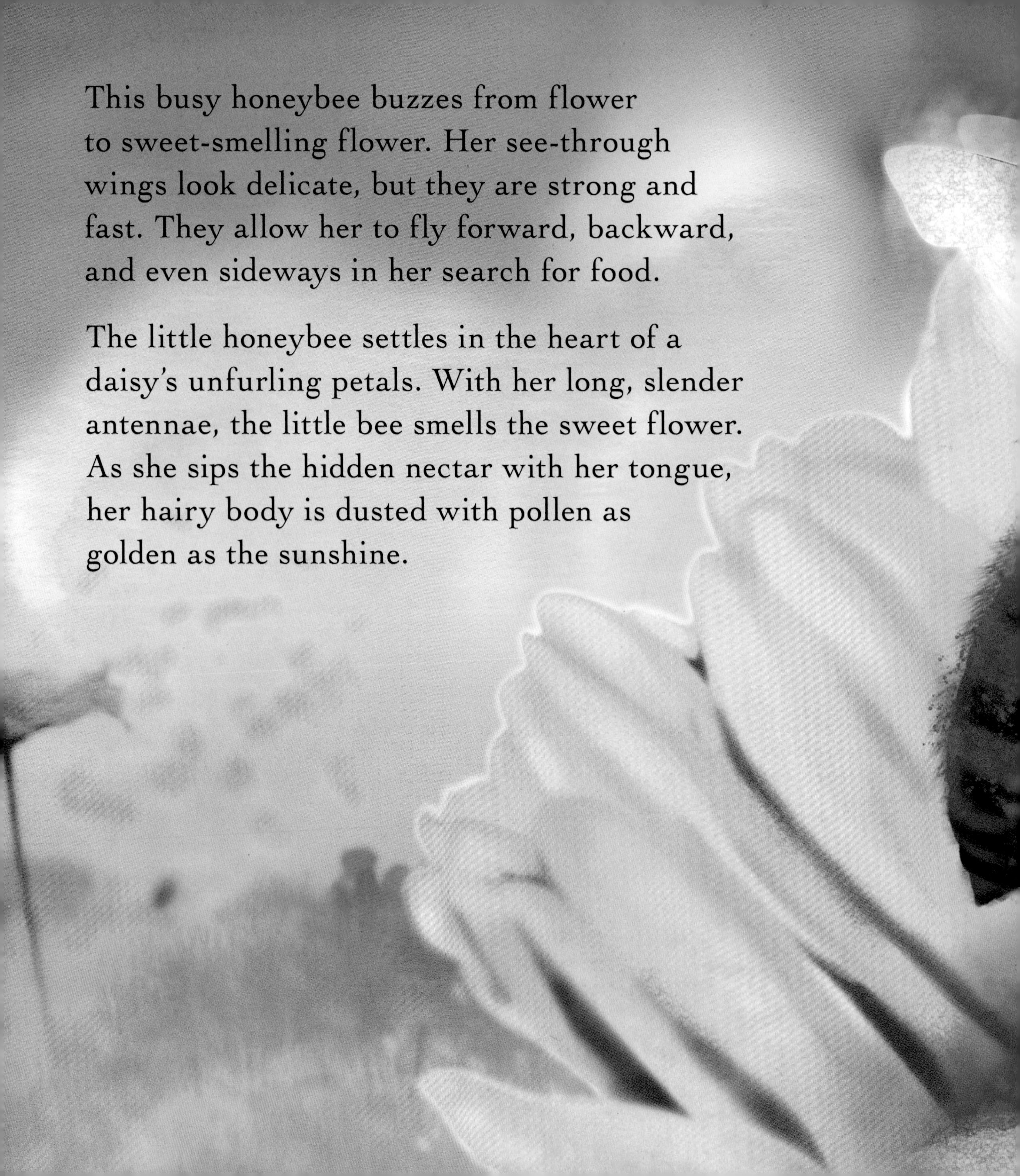

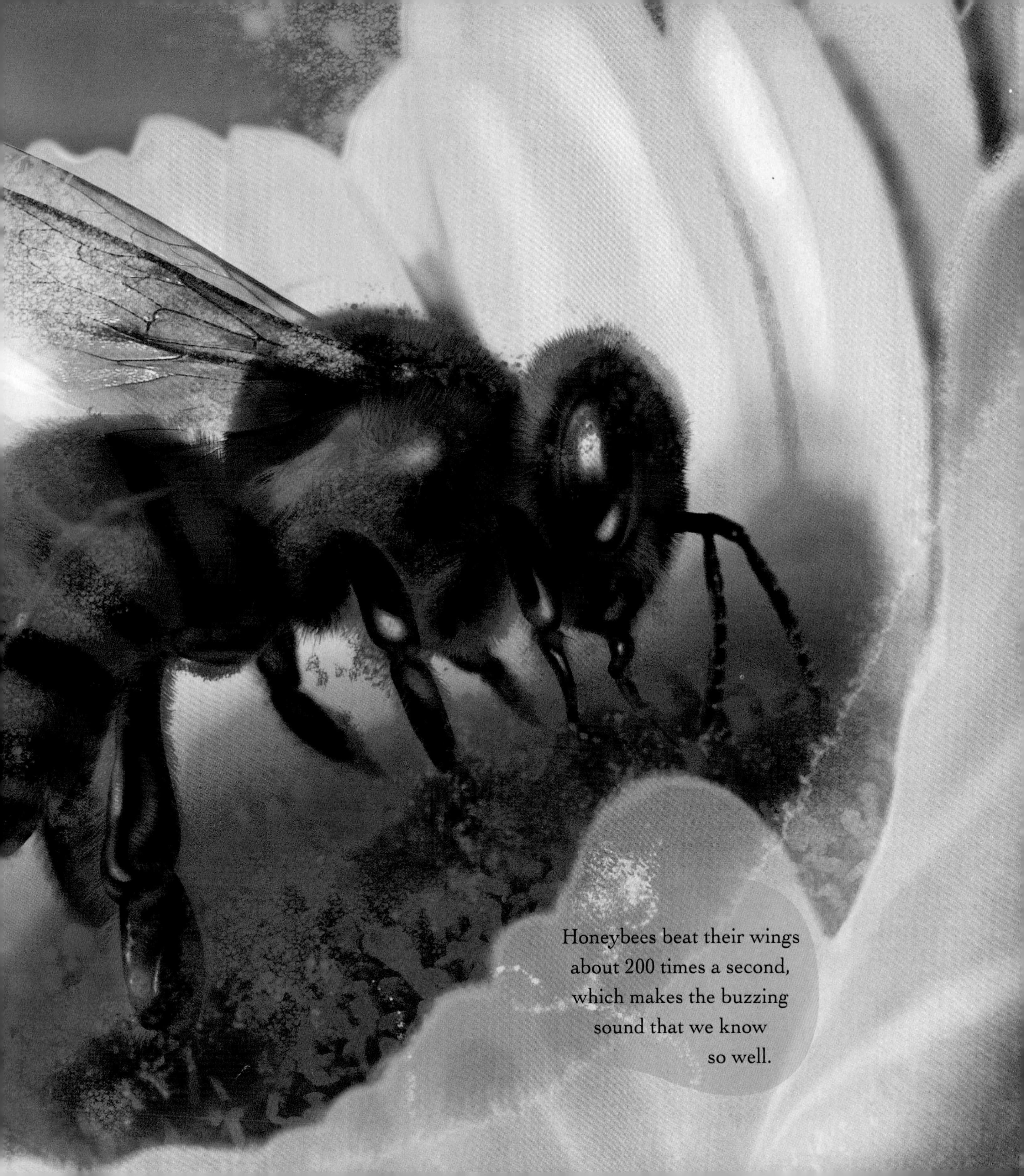

Honeybees beat their wings about 200 times a second, which makes the buzzing sound that we know so well.

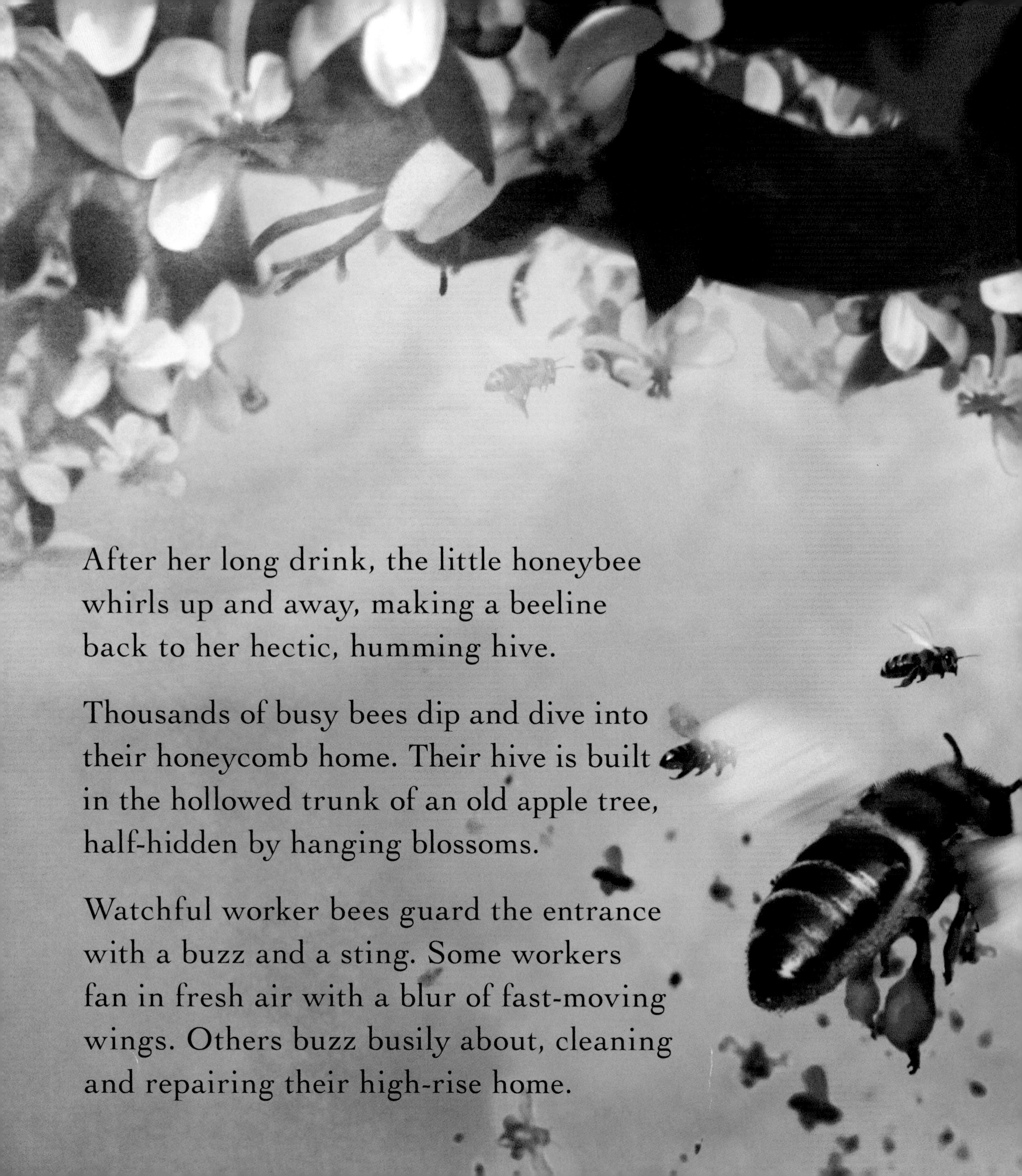

After her long drink, the little honeybee whirls up and away, making a beeline back to her hectic, humming hive.

Thousands of busy bees dip and dive into their honeycomb home. Their hive is built in the hollowed trunk of an old apple tree, half-hidden by hanging blossoms.

Watchful worker bees guard the entrance with a buzz and a sting. Some workers fan in fresh air with a blur of fast-moving wings. Others buzz busily about, cleaning and repairing their high-rise home.

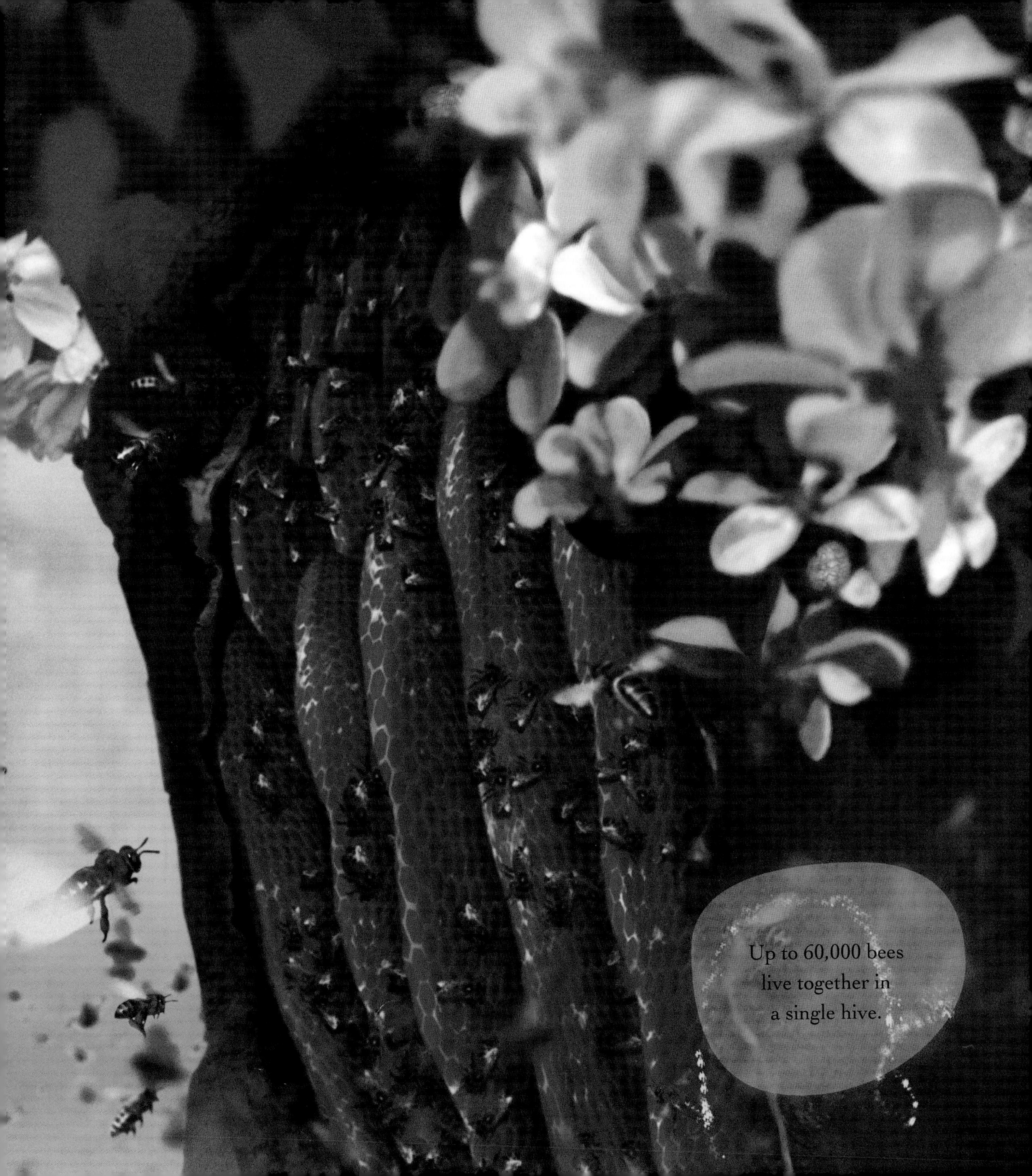

Up to 60,000 bees
live together in
a single hive.

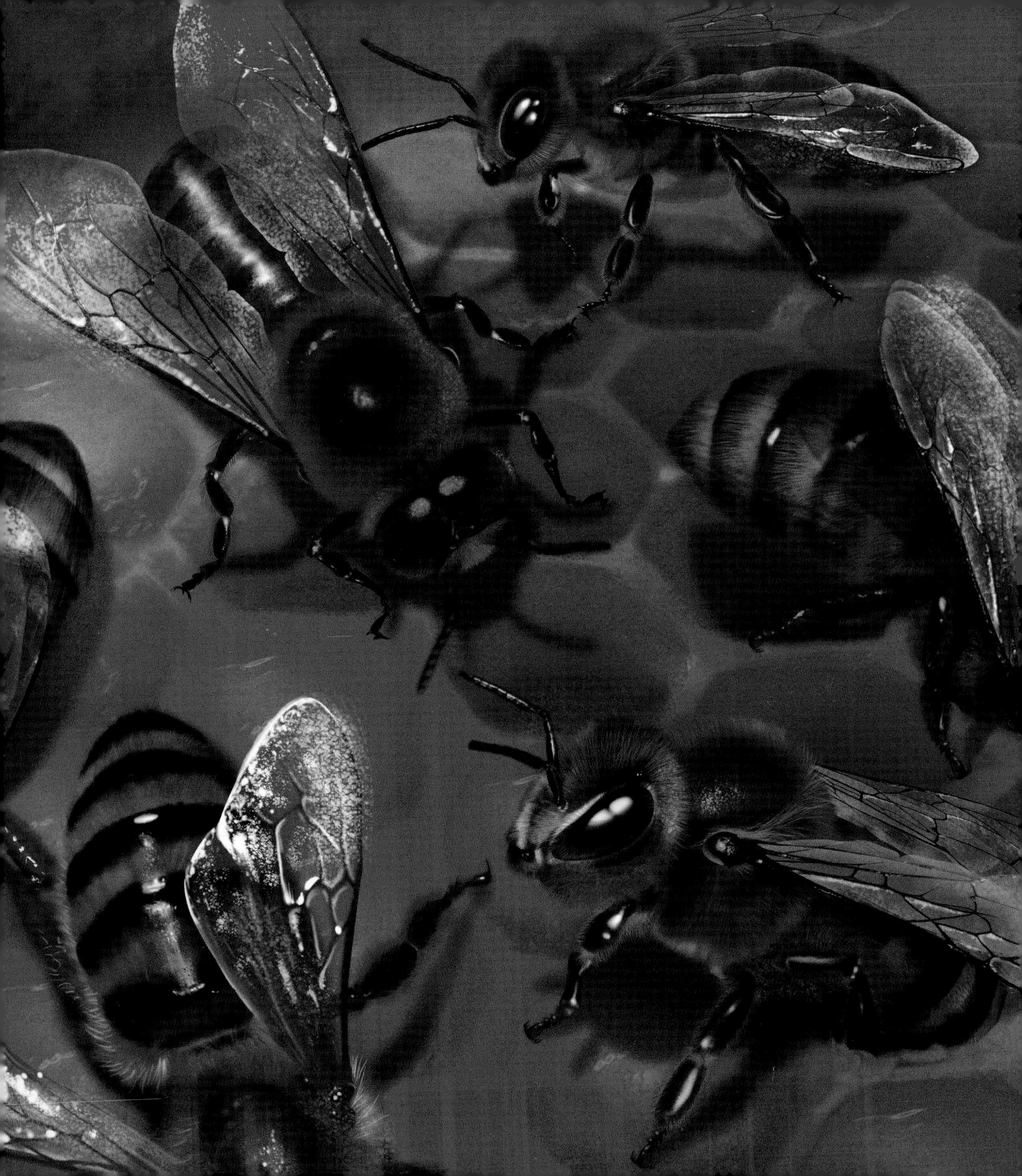

The little honeybee lives with thousands of other bees. The golden hive is her home. The busy bees are her family.

Most are worker bees, like she is. But the bigger, male bees are drones, and the biggest bee of all is a queen.

Each bee has a job to do. The workers build a honeycomb nest in the hidden heart of the hive. The queen bee's babies will feed on honey-nectar here. They will grow and change inside the colony's secret six-sided cells.

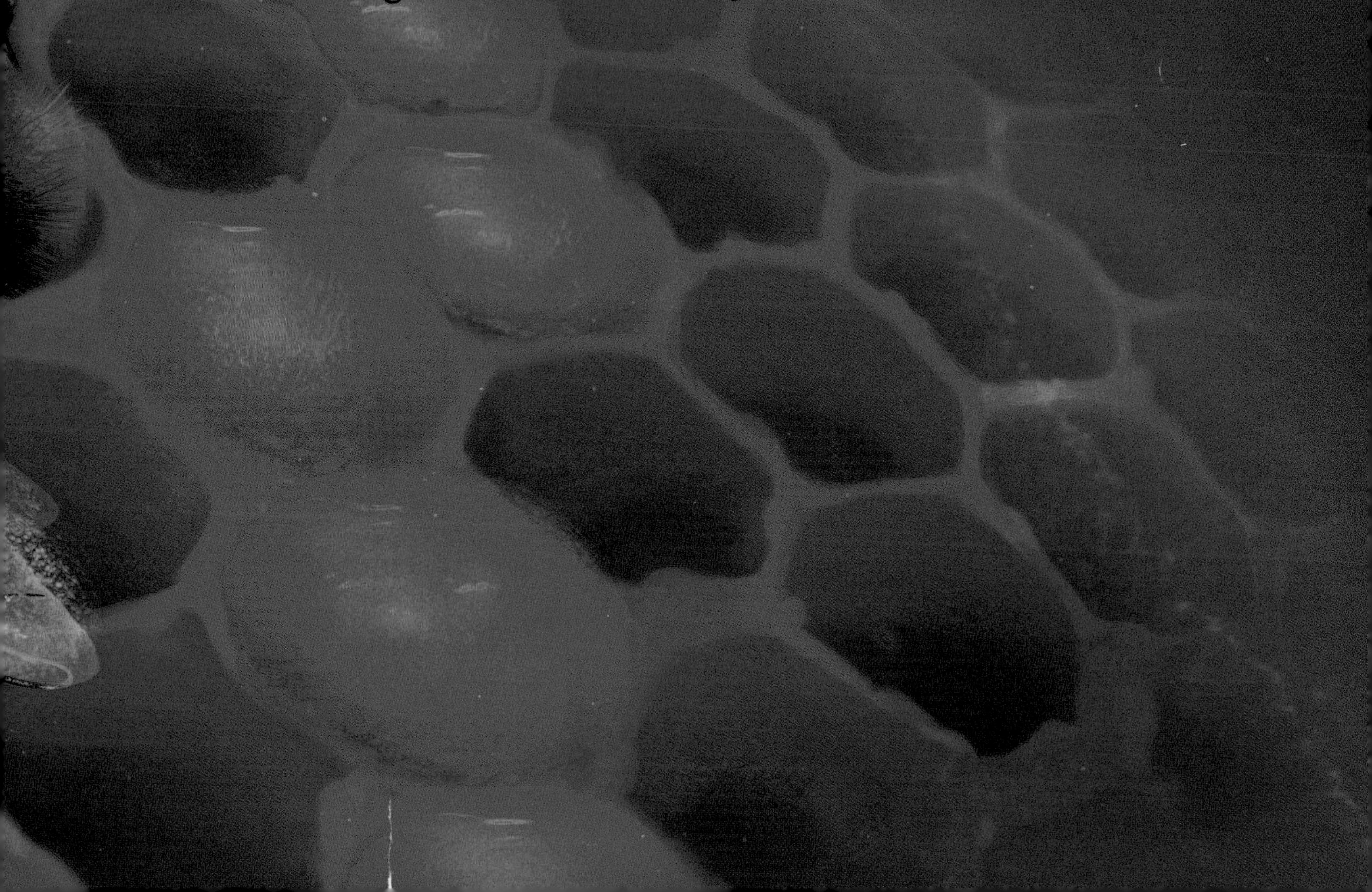

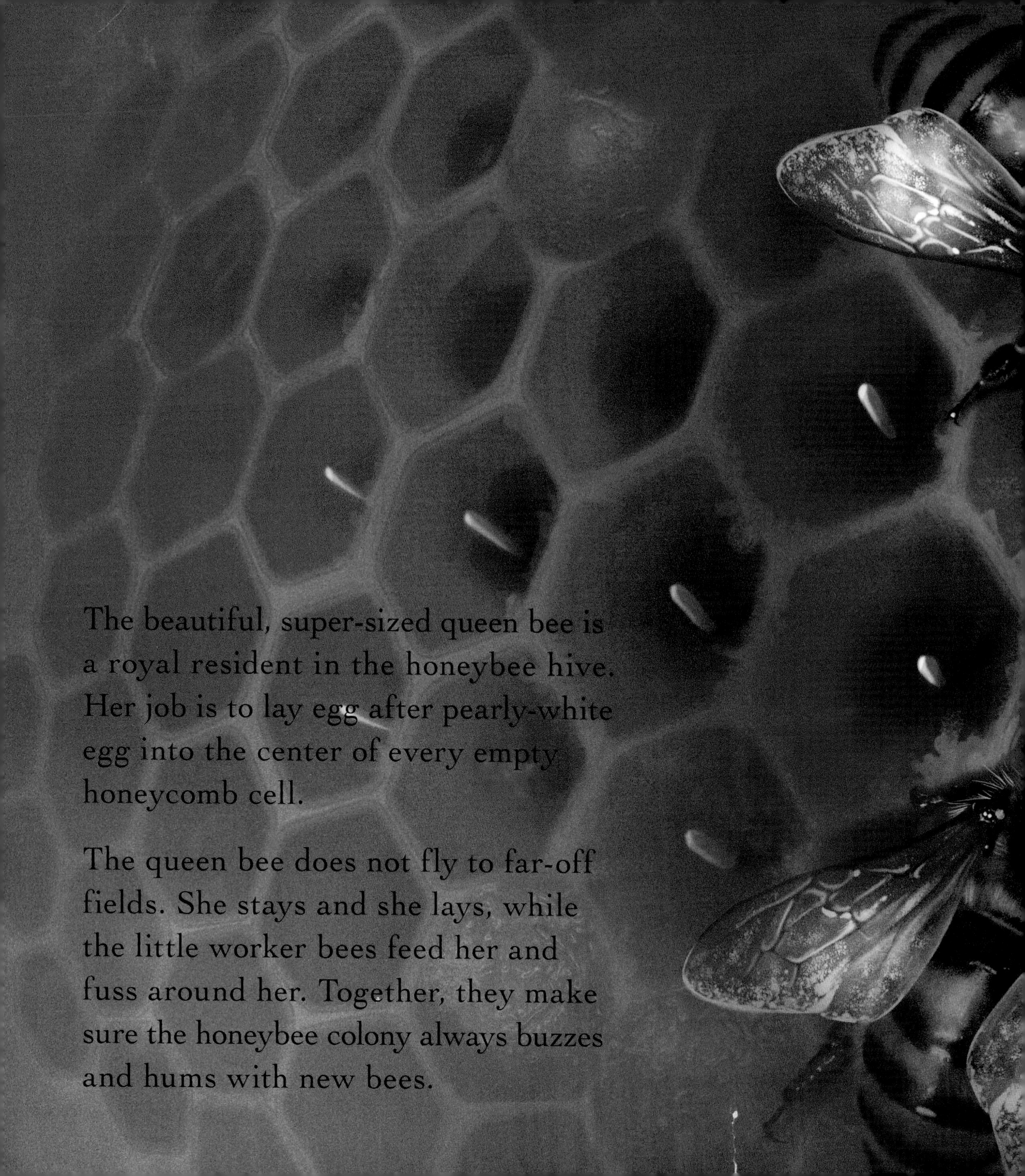

The beautiful, super-sized queen bee is a royal resident in the honeybee hive. Her job is to lay egg after pearly-white egg into the center of every empty honeycomb cell.

The queen bee does not fly to far-off fields. She stays and she lays, while the little worker bees feed her and fuss around her. Together, they make sure the honeybee colony always buzzes and hums with new bees.

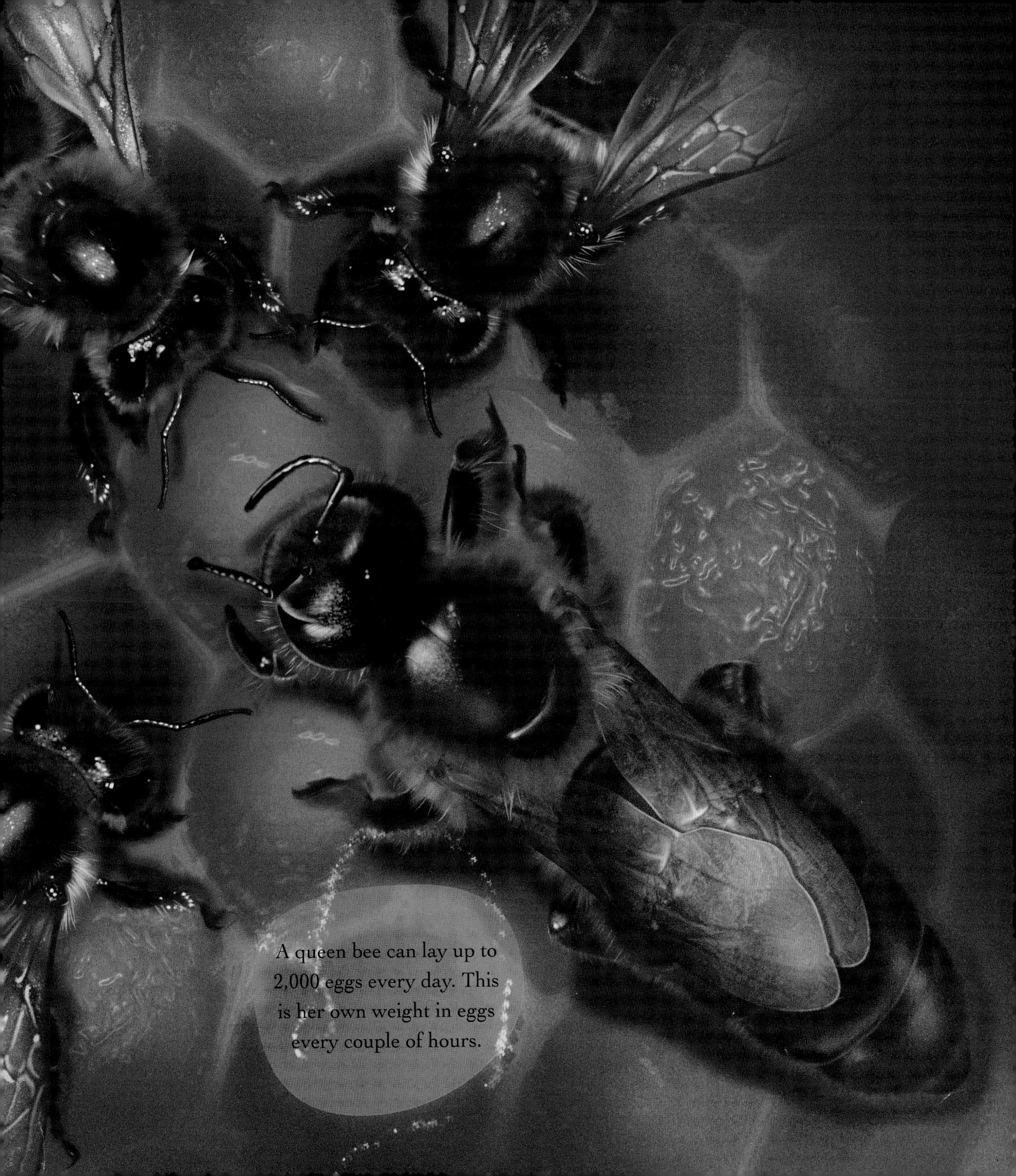

A queen bee can lay up to 2,000 eggs every day. This is her own weight in eggs every couple of hours.

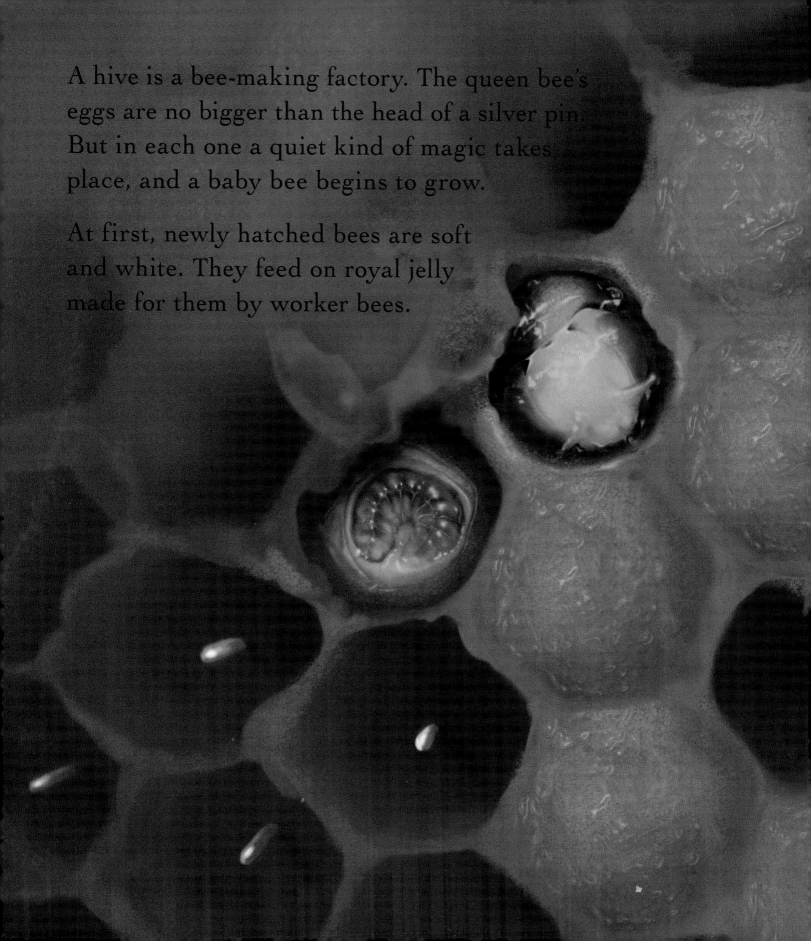

A hive is a bee-making factory. The queen bee's eggs are no bigger than the head of a silver pin. But in each one a quiet kind of magic takes place, and a baby bee begins to grow.

At first, newly hatched bees are soft and white. They feed on royal jelly made for them by worker bees.

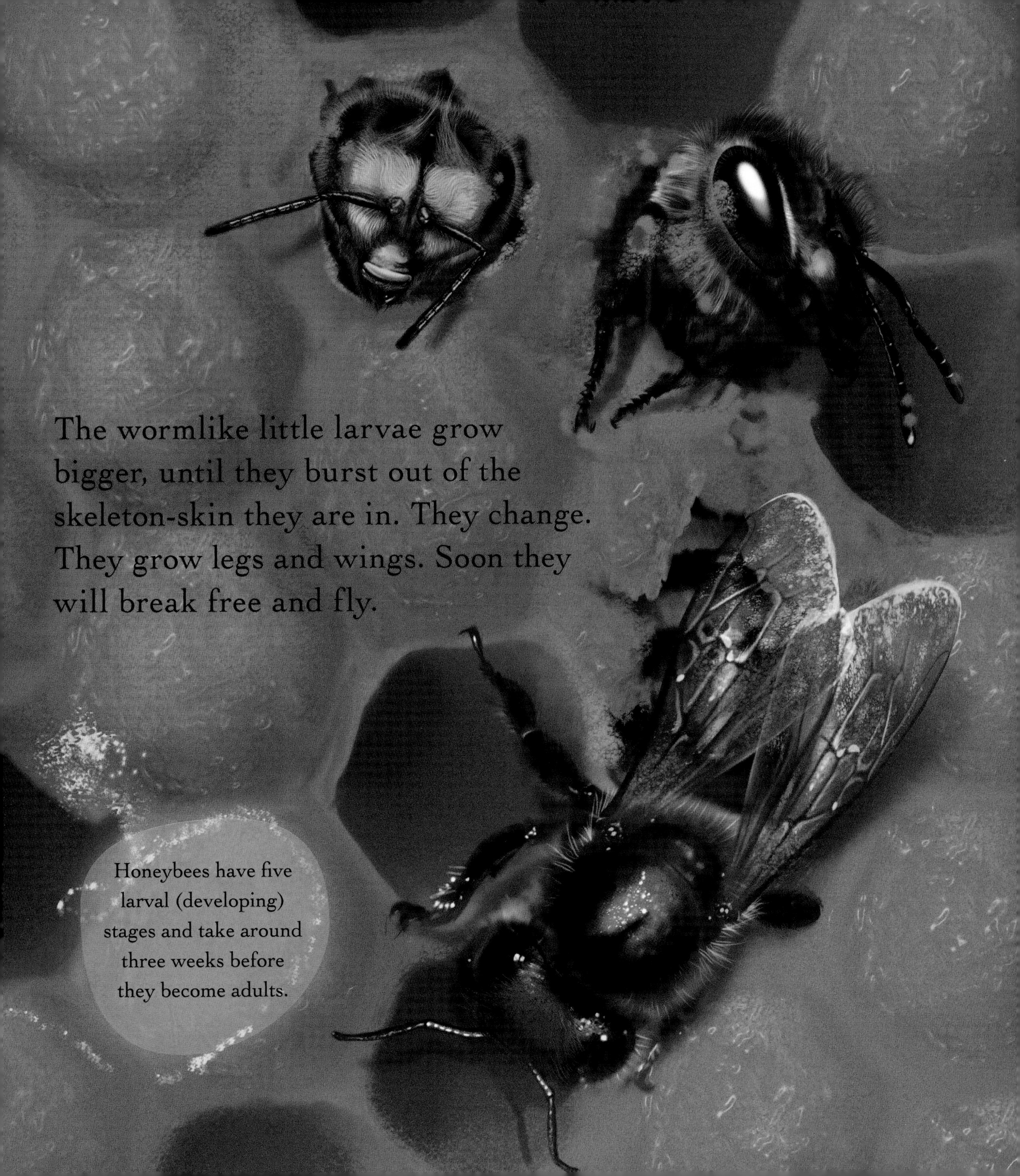

The wormlike little larvae grow bigger, until they burst out of the skeleton-skin they are in. They change. They grow legs and wings. Soon they will break free and fly.

Honeybees have five larval (developing) stages and take around three weeks before they become adults.

Worker bees gather the food that fuels the hive. In fine weather, the older bees fly far and wide to forage in fields and sip from flowers.

The bees see the striking patterns and many of the bright colors in flowers. They smell the nectar and the pollen. The flowers invite them to come close.

The little honeybee hovers like a helicopter above a flower's pink petals. She lands lightly. She drinks deeply. Inside a special part of her stomach, the sugary nectar begins to turn into honey for the hive.

Worker bees can travel up to 500 miles during their foraging lifetime of 17 days.

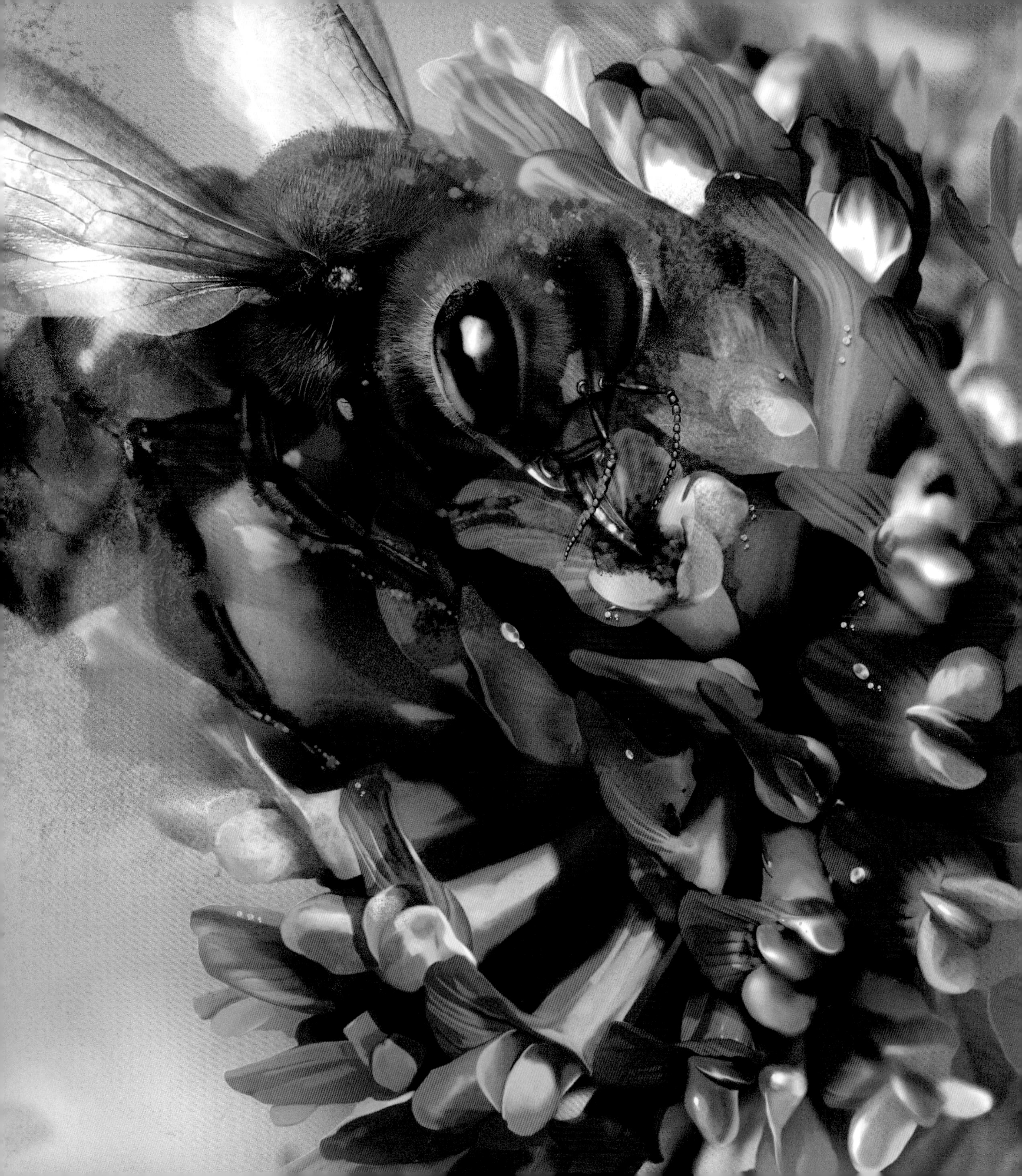

The little honeybee does not rest yet. She lands in a puff of pollen, rolling the round, golden grains into tiny baskets on her back legs. The sticky pollen clings to her hairy body, dusting her black stripes with gold.

The little honeybee clambers and climbs. She flits and sips. As she moves, she mixes pollen from flower to flower. Because of her work, seeds will form and new plants will grow.

Foraging worker bees make about 10 trips to and from the hive, and visit about 100 flowers each day.

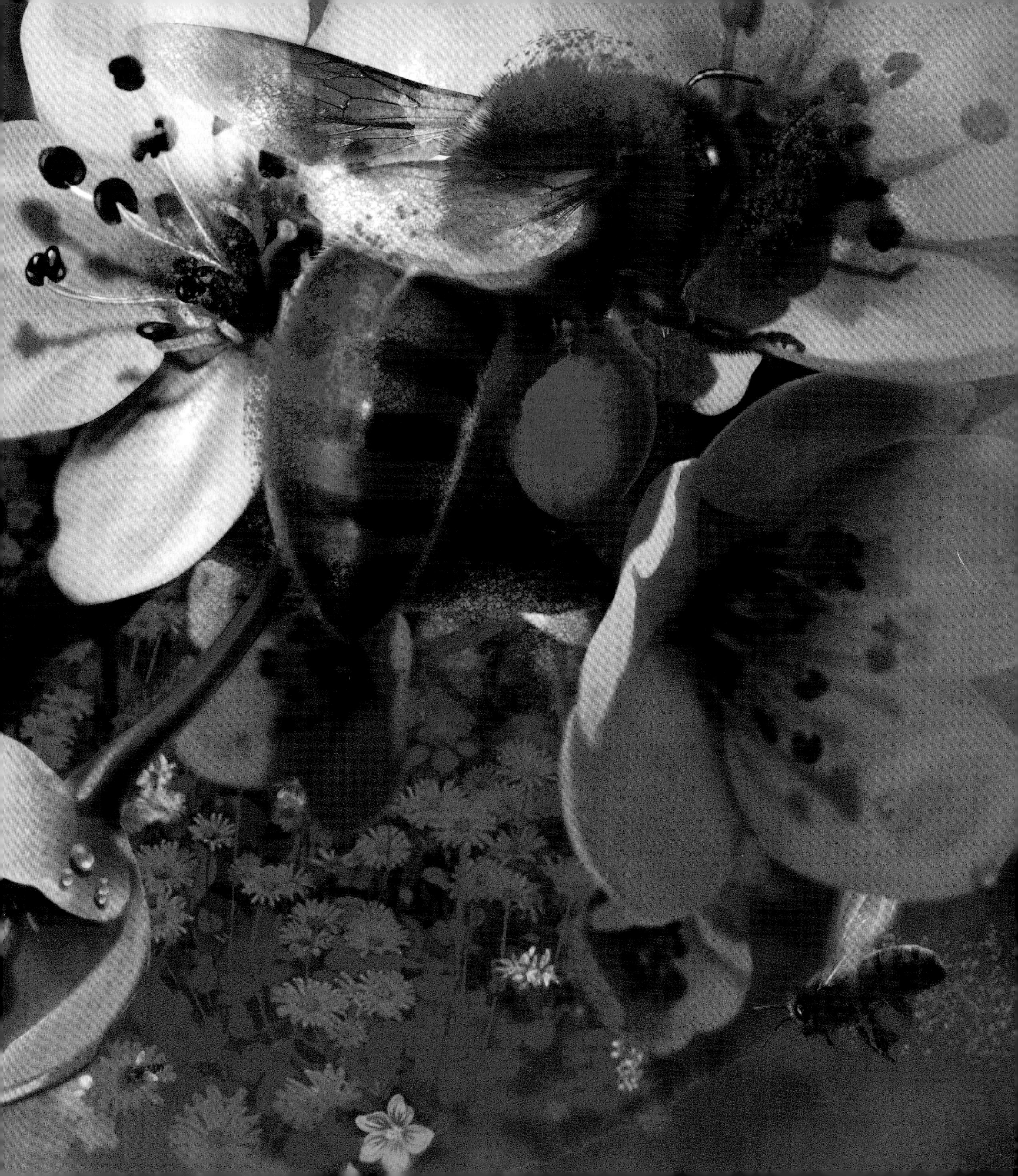

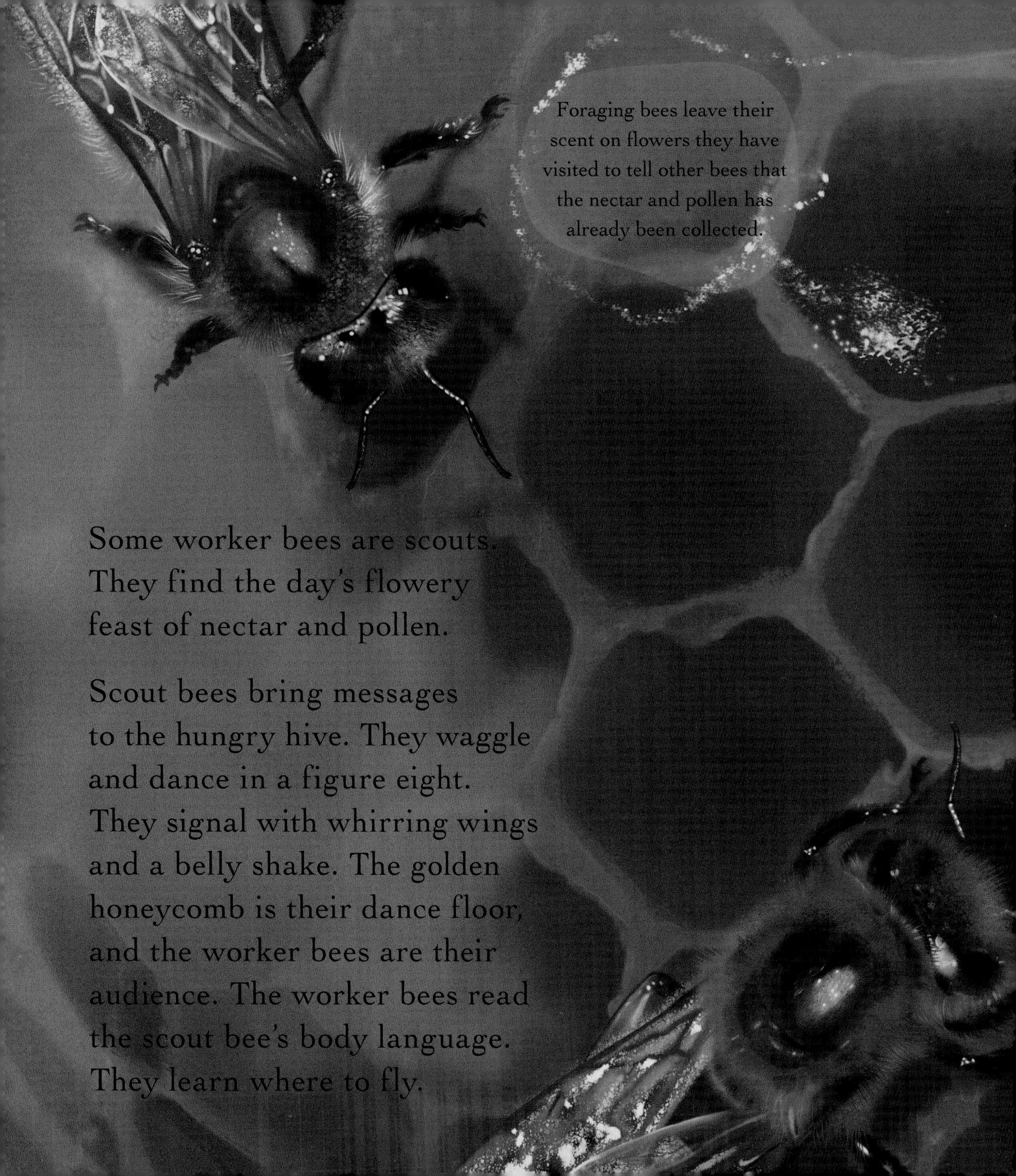

Foraging bees leave their scent on flowers they have visited to tell other bees that the nectar and pollen has already been collected.

Some worker bees are scouts. They find the day's flowery feast of nectar and pollen.

Scout bees bring messages to the hungry hive. They waggle and dance in a figure eight. They signal with whirring wings and a belly shake. The golden honeycomb is their dance floor, and the worker bees are their audience. The worker bees read the scout bee's body language. They learn where to fly.

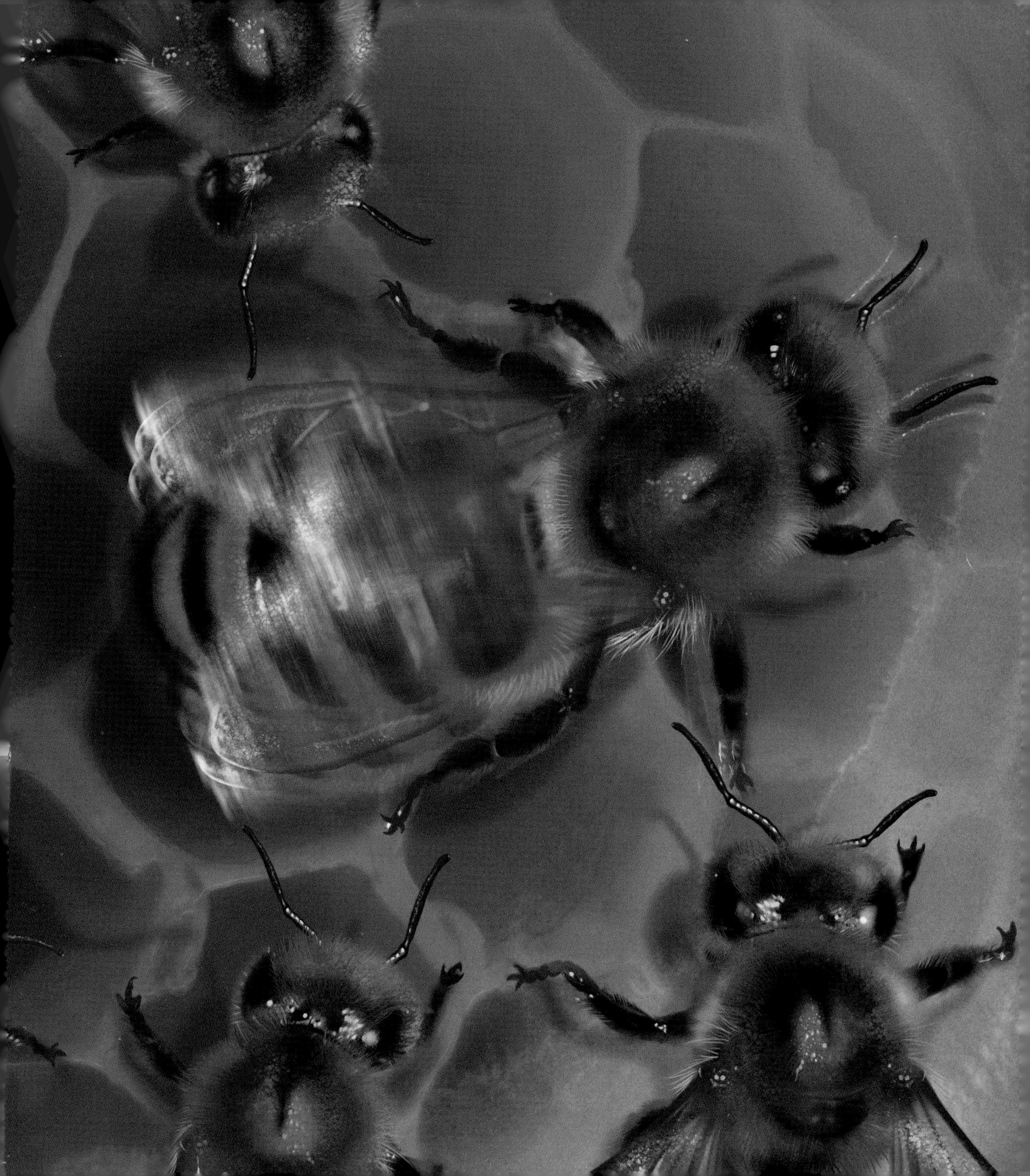

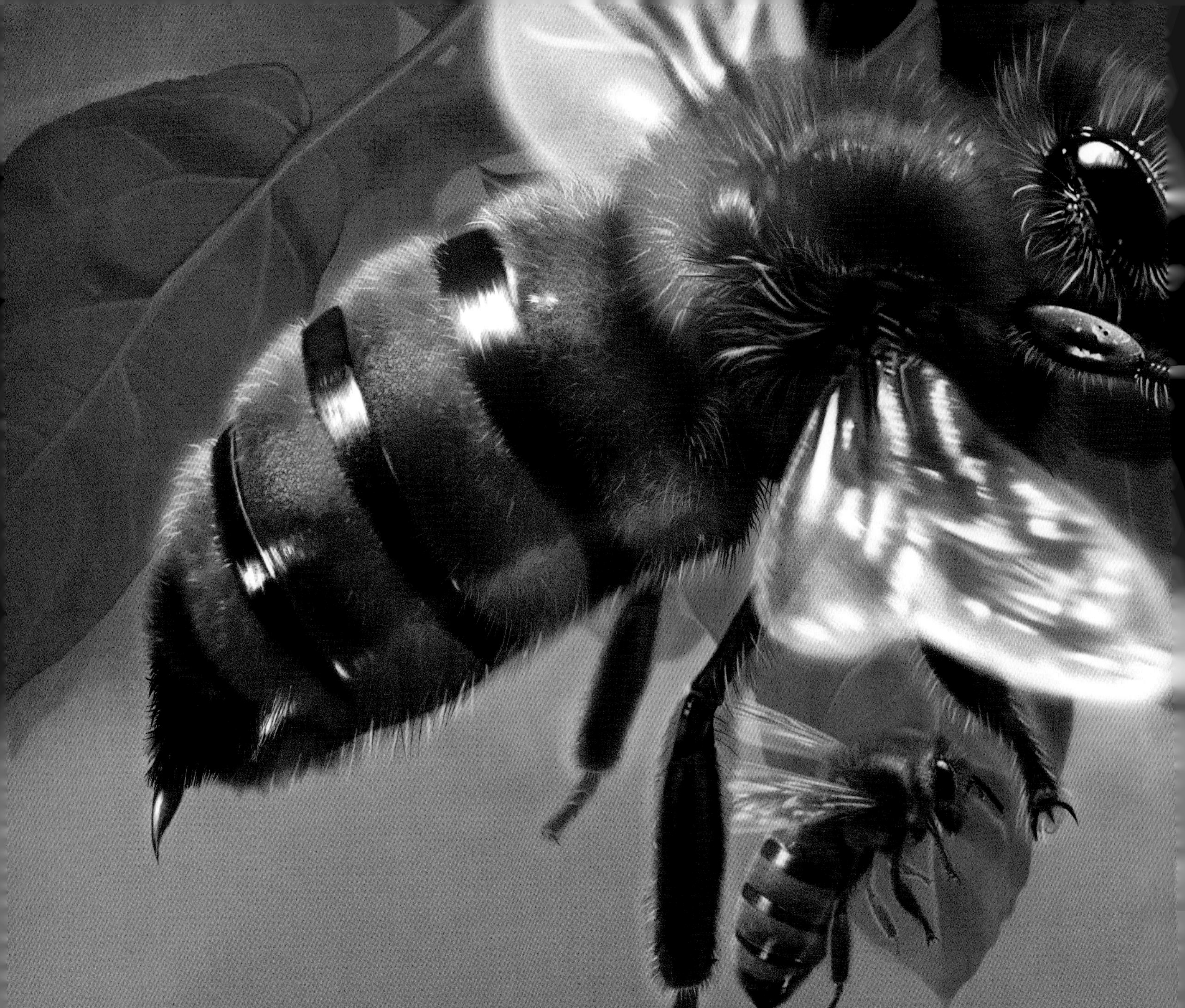

Worker bees can fight like warriors. They have a sharp, poison-filled sting to keep honey-snatchers away. Worker bees use their sting for defence, but it is a one-time weapon.

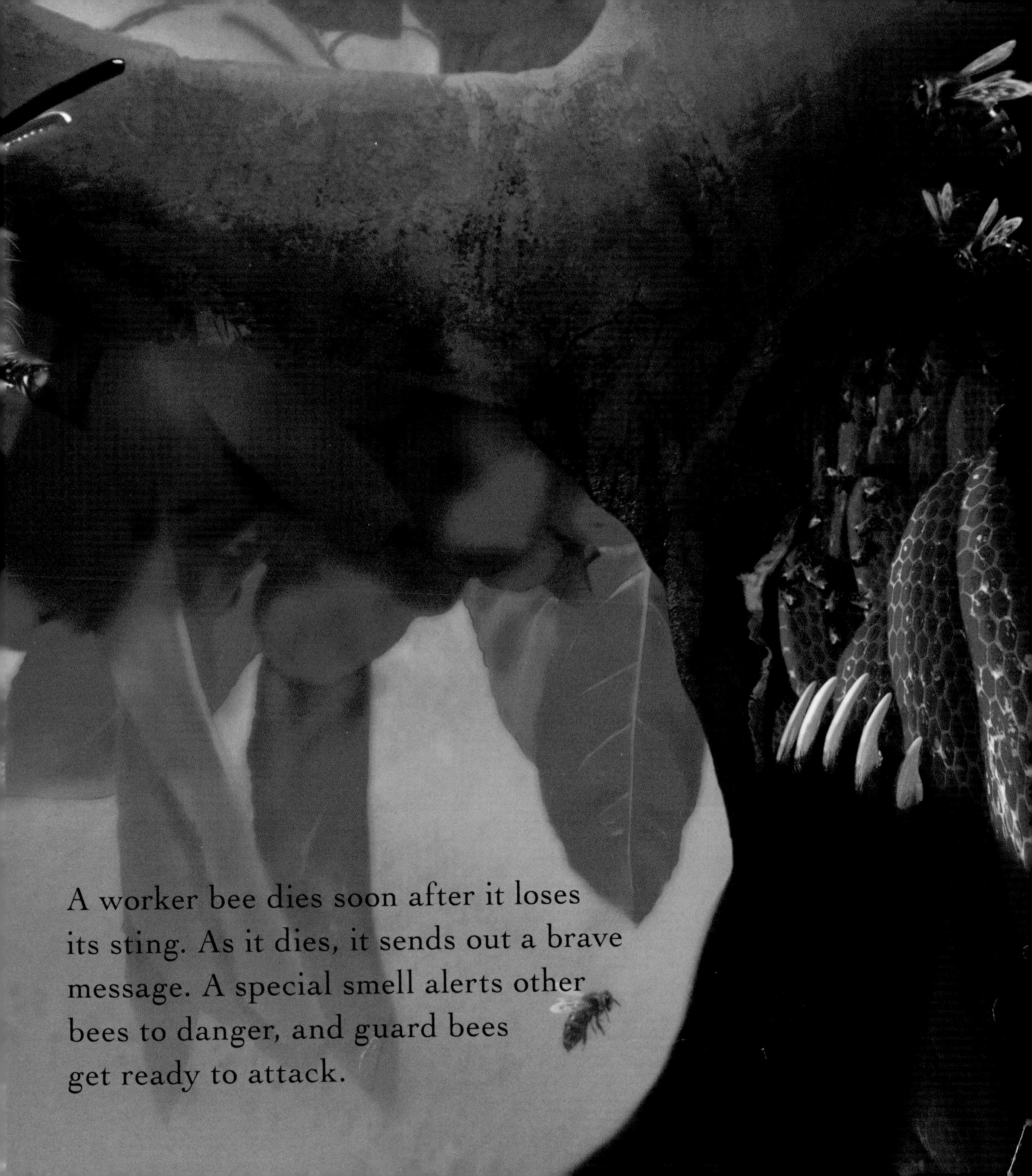

A worker bee dies soon after it loses its sting. As it dies, it sends out a brave message. A special smell alerts other bees to danger, and guard bees get ready to attack.

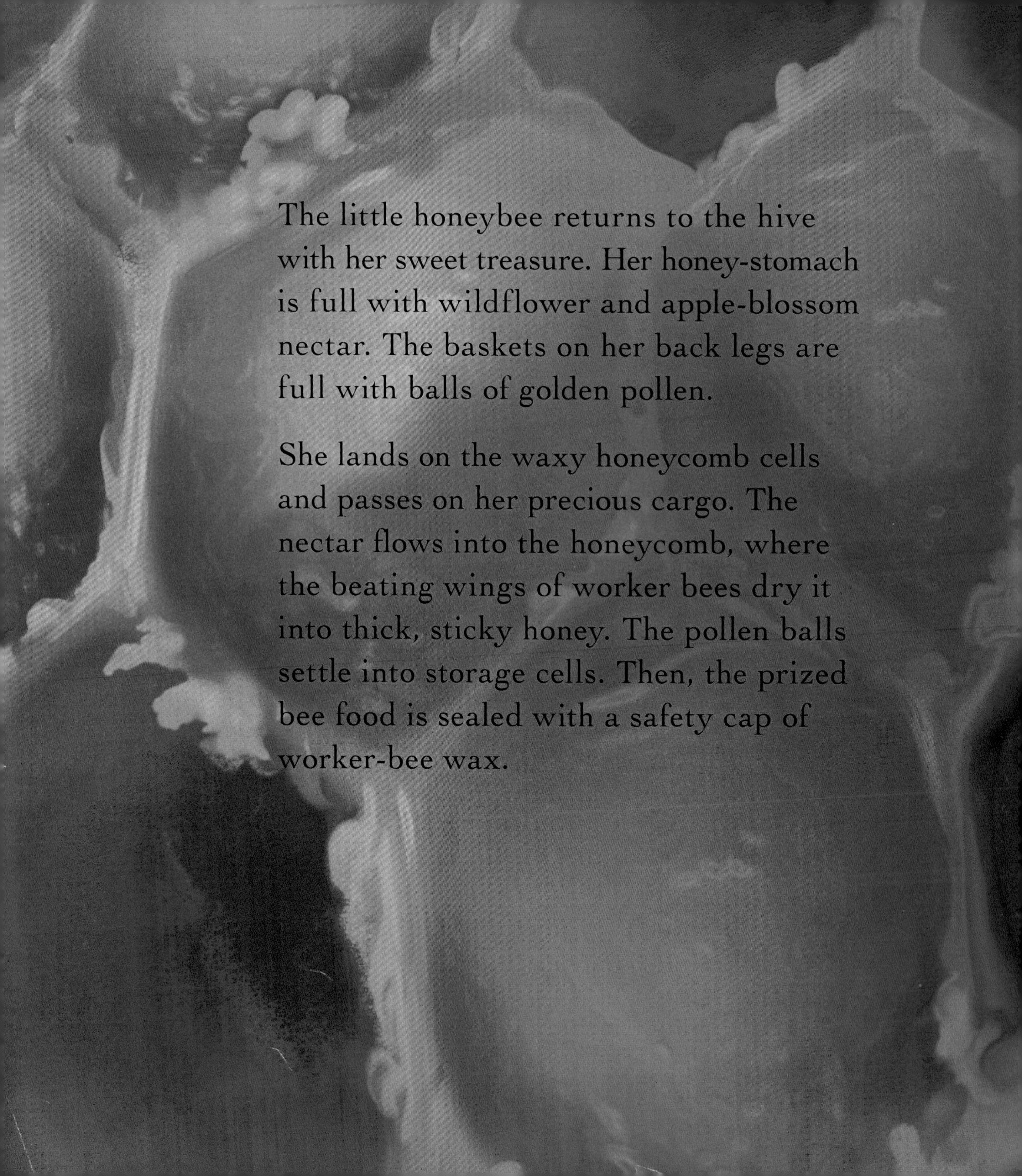

The little honeybee returns to the hive with her sweet treasure. Her honey-stomach is full with wildflower and apple-blossom nectar. The baskets on her back legs are full with balls of golden pollen.

She lands on the waxy honeycomb cells and passes on her precious cargo. The nectar flows into the honeycomb, where the beating wings of worker bees dry it into thick, sticky honey. The pollen balls settle into storage cells. Then, the prized bee food is sealed with a safety cap of worker-bee wax.

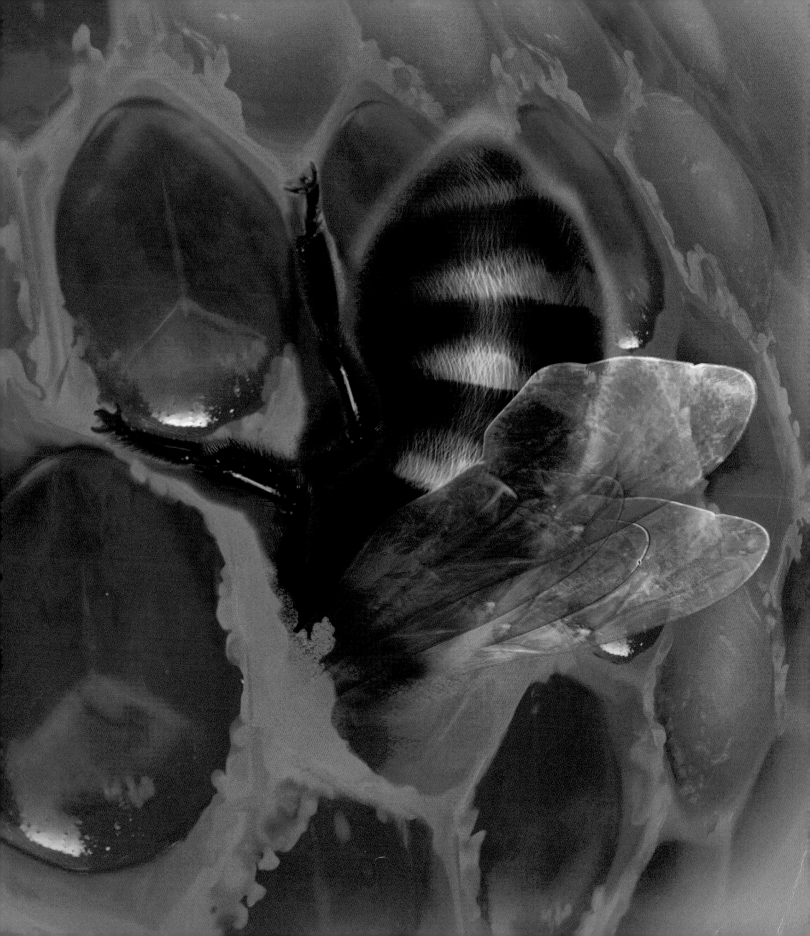

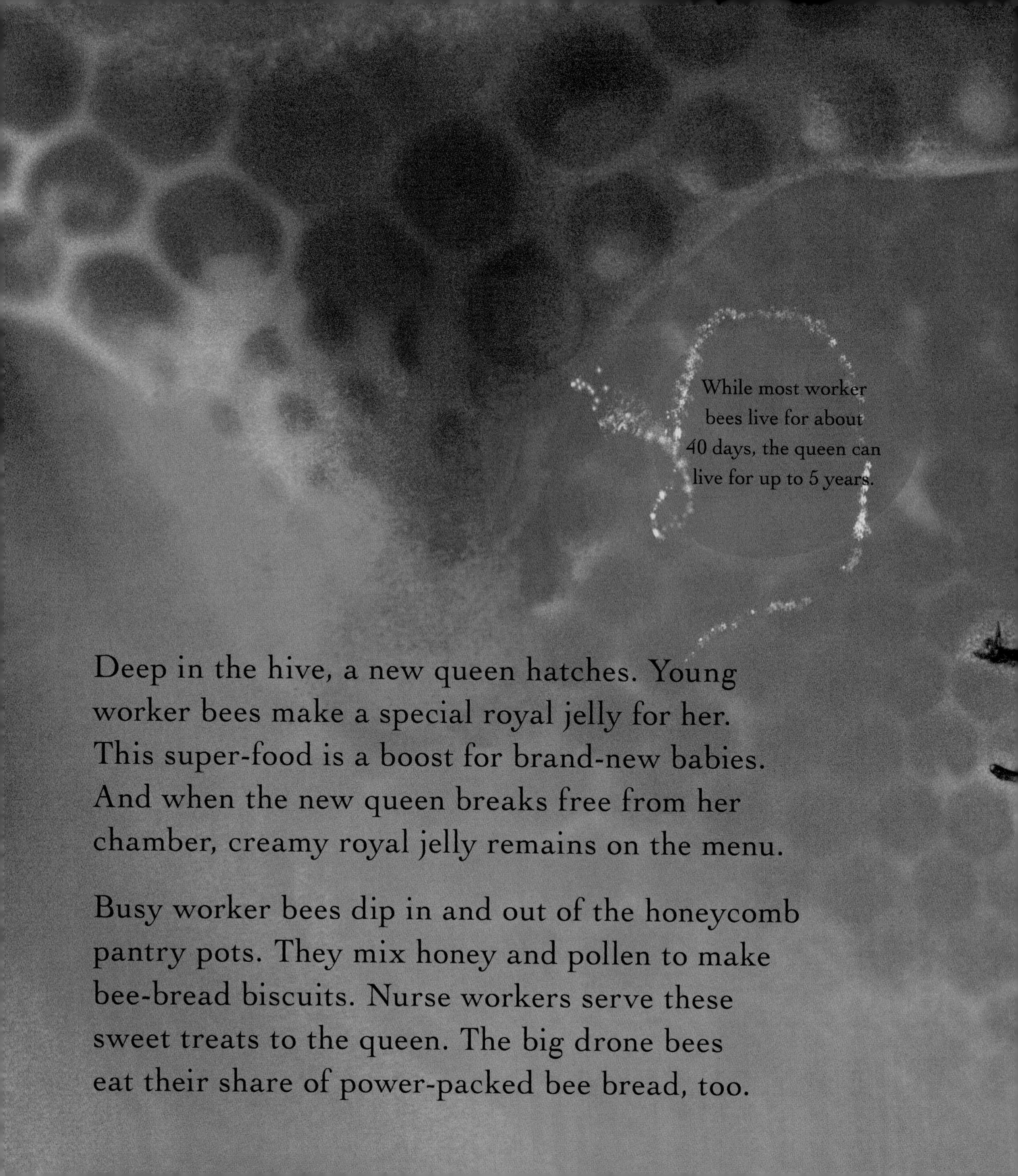

While most worker bees live for about 40 days, the queen can live for up to 5 years.

Deep in the hive, a new queen hatches. Young worker bees make a special royal jelly for her. This super-food is a boost for brand-new babies. And when the new queen breaks free from her chamber, creamy royal jelly remains on the menu.

Busy worker bees dip in and out of the honeycomb pantry pots. They mix honey and pollen to make bee-bread biscuits. Nurse workers serve these sweet treats to the queen. The big drone bees eat their share of power-packed bee bread, too.

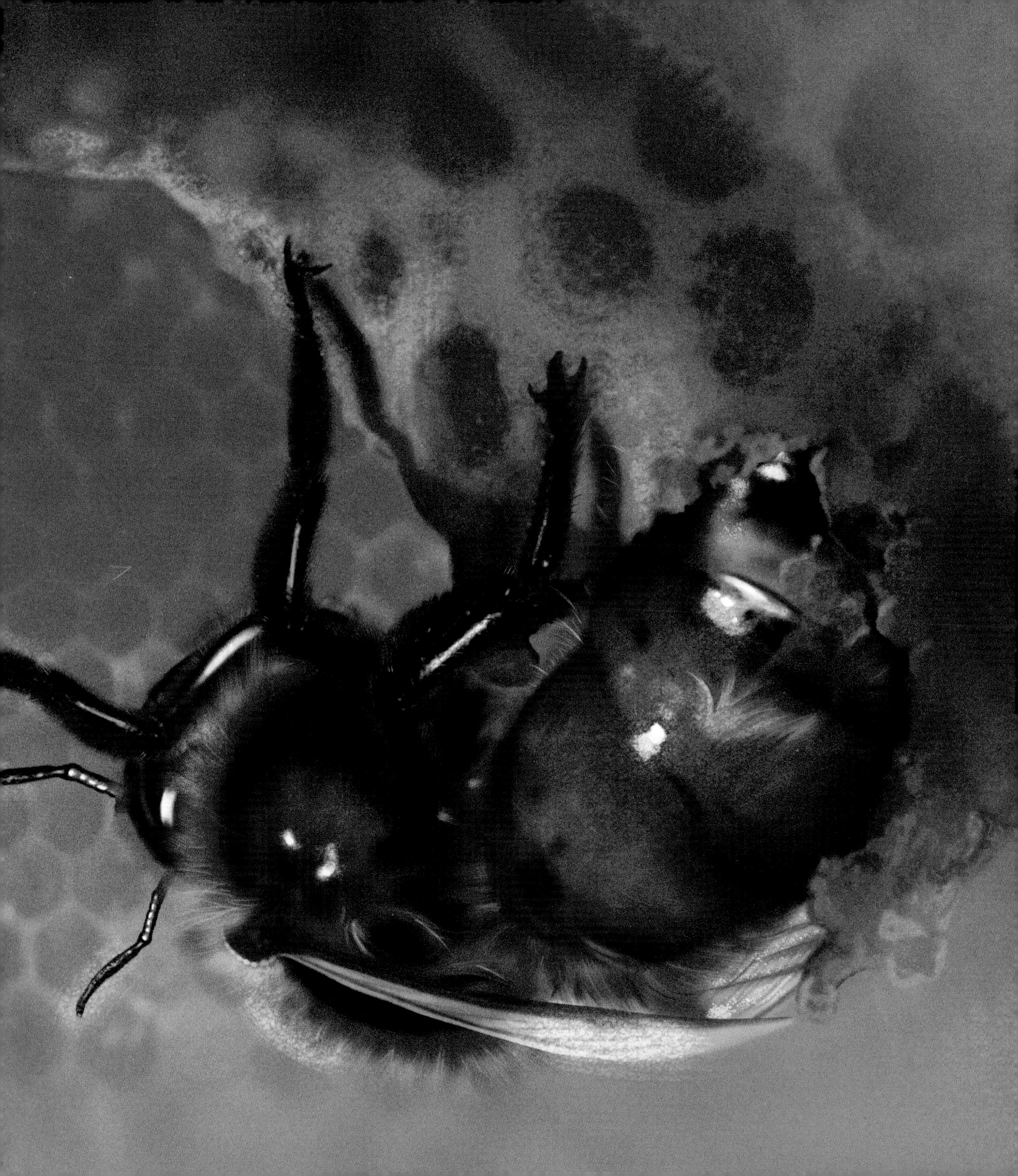

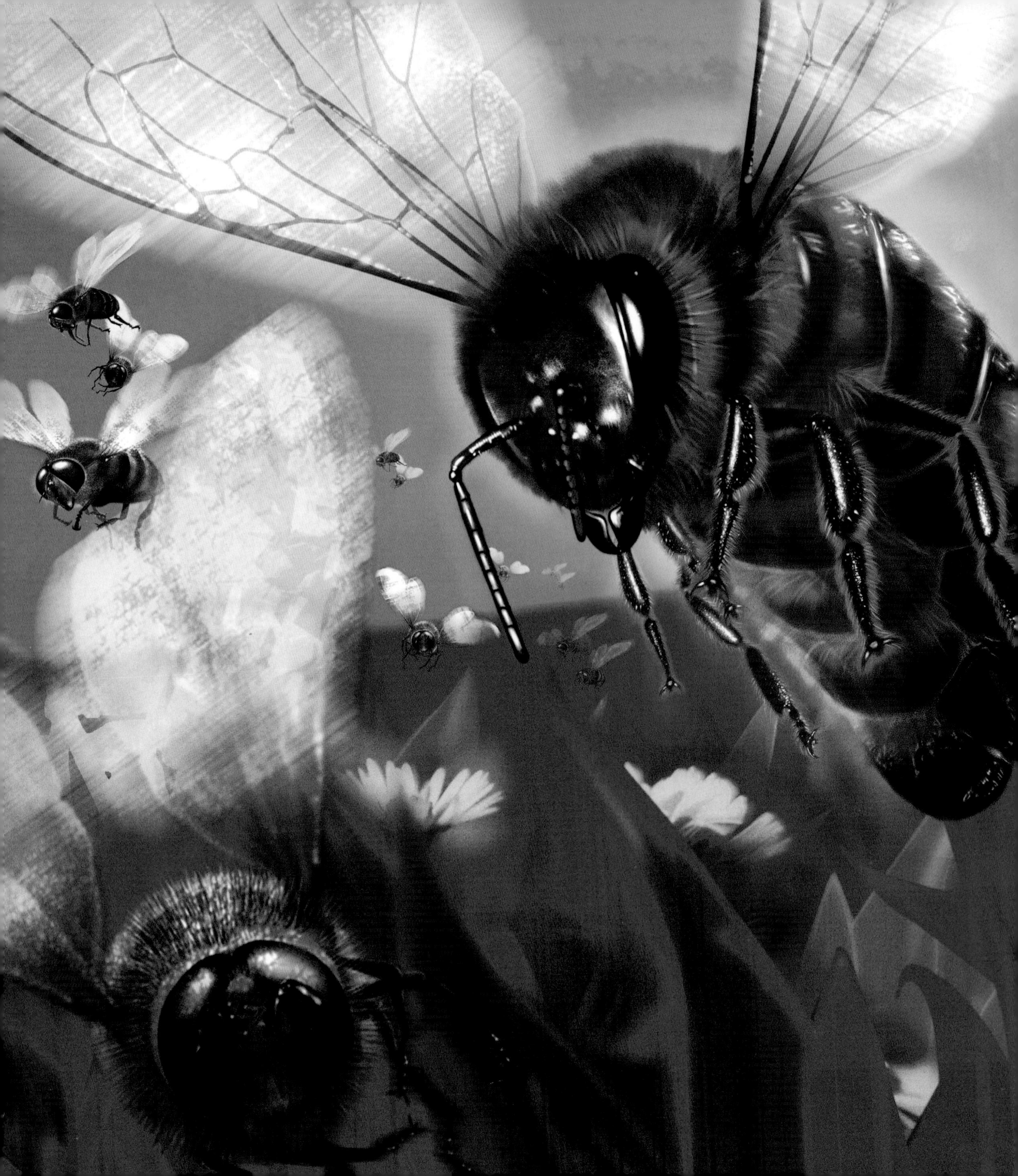

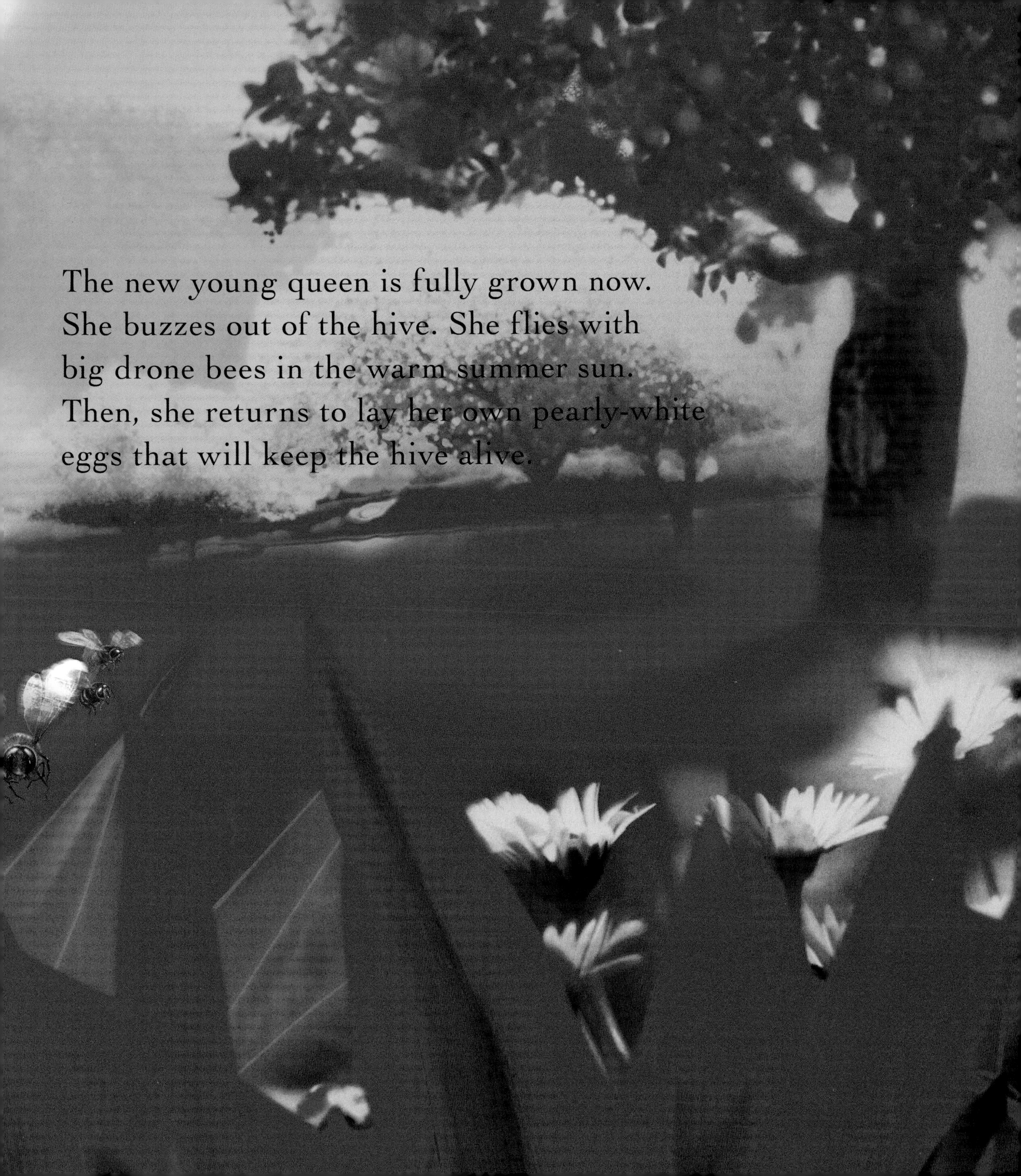

The new young queen is fully grown now. She buzzes out of the hive. She flies with big drone bees in the warm summer sun. Then, she returns to lay her own pearly-white eggs that will keep the hive alive.

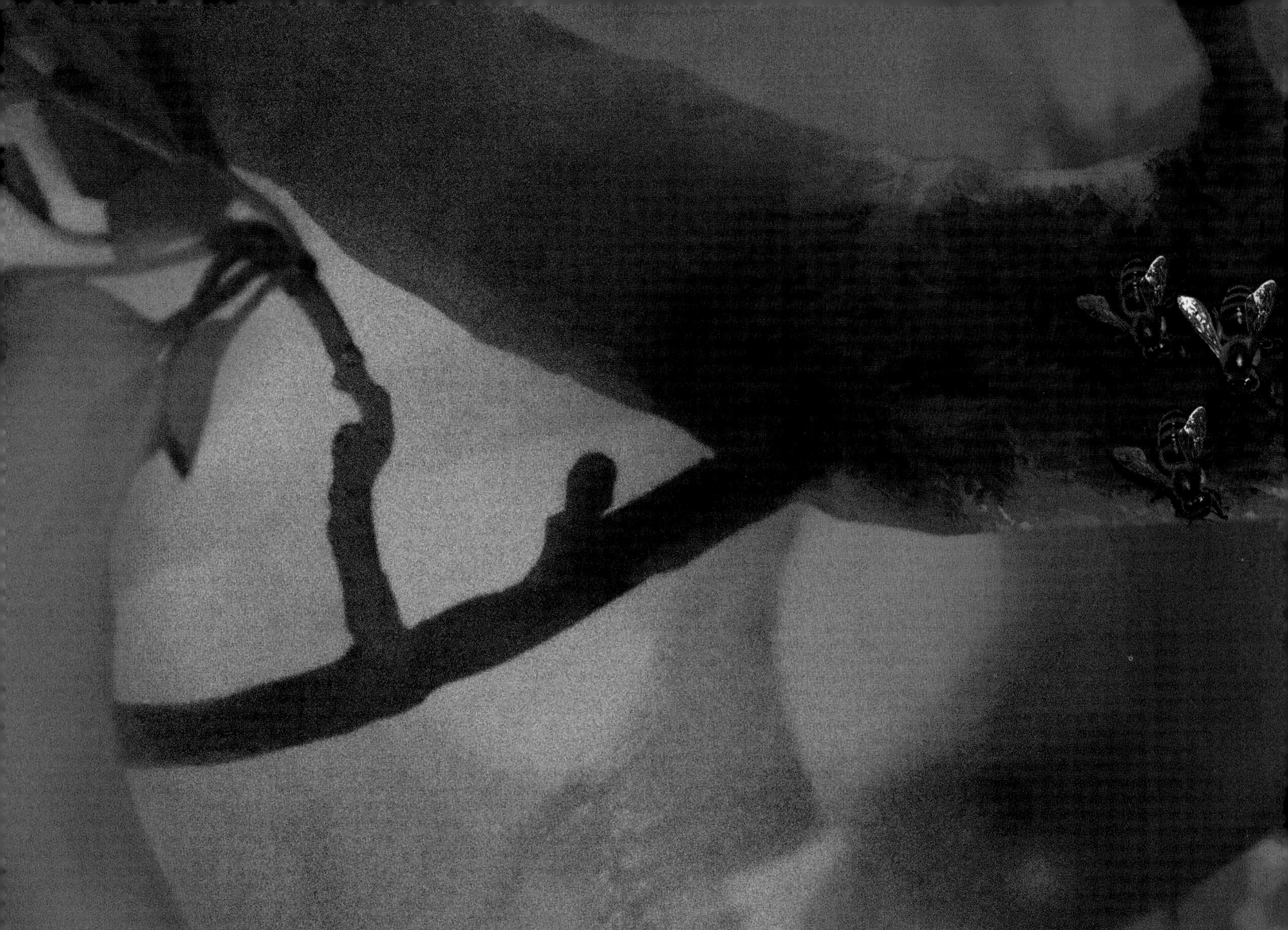

The hive is getting bigger and busier. It is time for the old queen to start a new hive. A shield of worker bees surrounds her in a tightly swirling swarm. Together they fly away from the old hive like a buzzing dark cloud.

While scout bees seek a site to build a new home, the old queen and her guards rest on the branch of a gnarly apple tree.

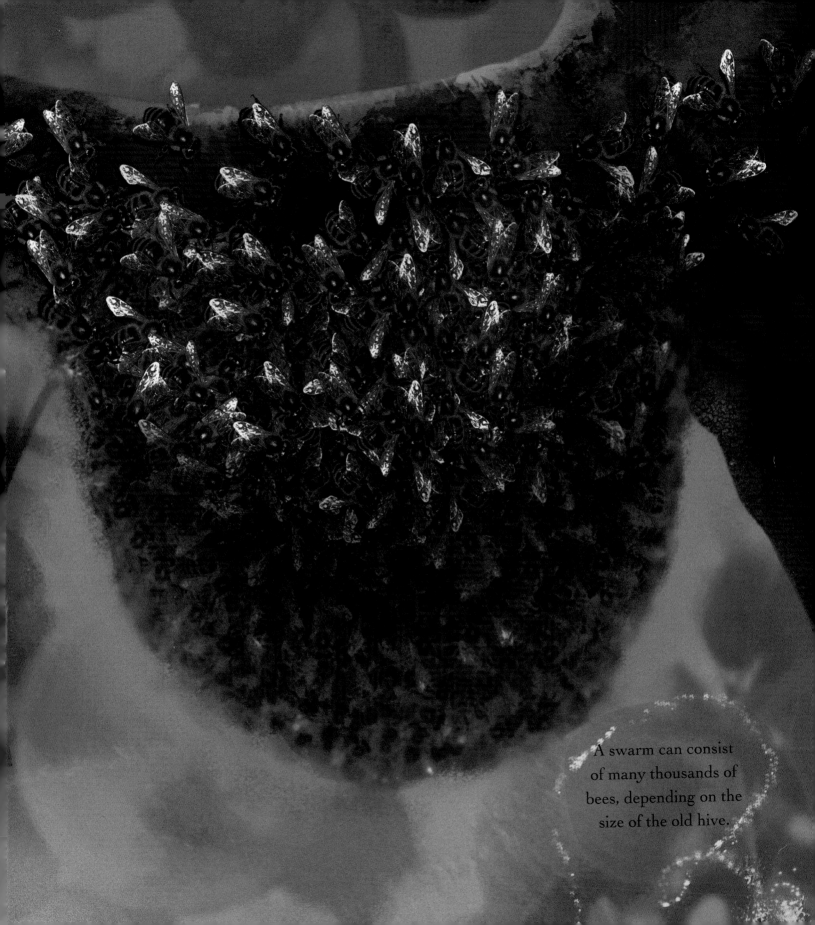

A swarm can consist
of many thousands of
bees, depending on the
size of the old hive.

The little honeybee stays with the young queen and her hive in the old apple tree. She has flown far and worked hard over the long, sunlit days of summer. But seasons change and hard times come.

In the chill of winter, the bees huddle in their hive, shivering and shaking. They crowd together to keep heat from escaping. They sip from their store of sweet honey and golden pollen.

The honeybees worked together to build their hive and gather their food. Together they survive the dark winter and emerge when new spring flowers bloom.

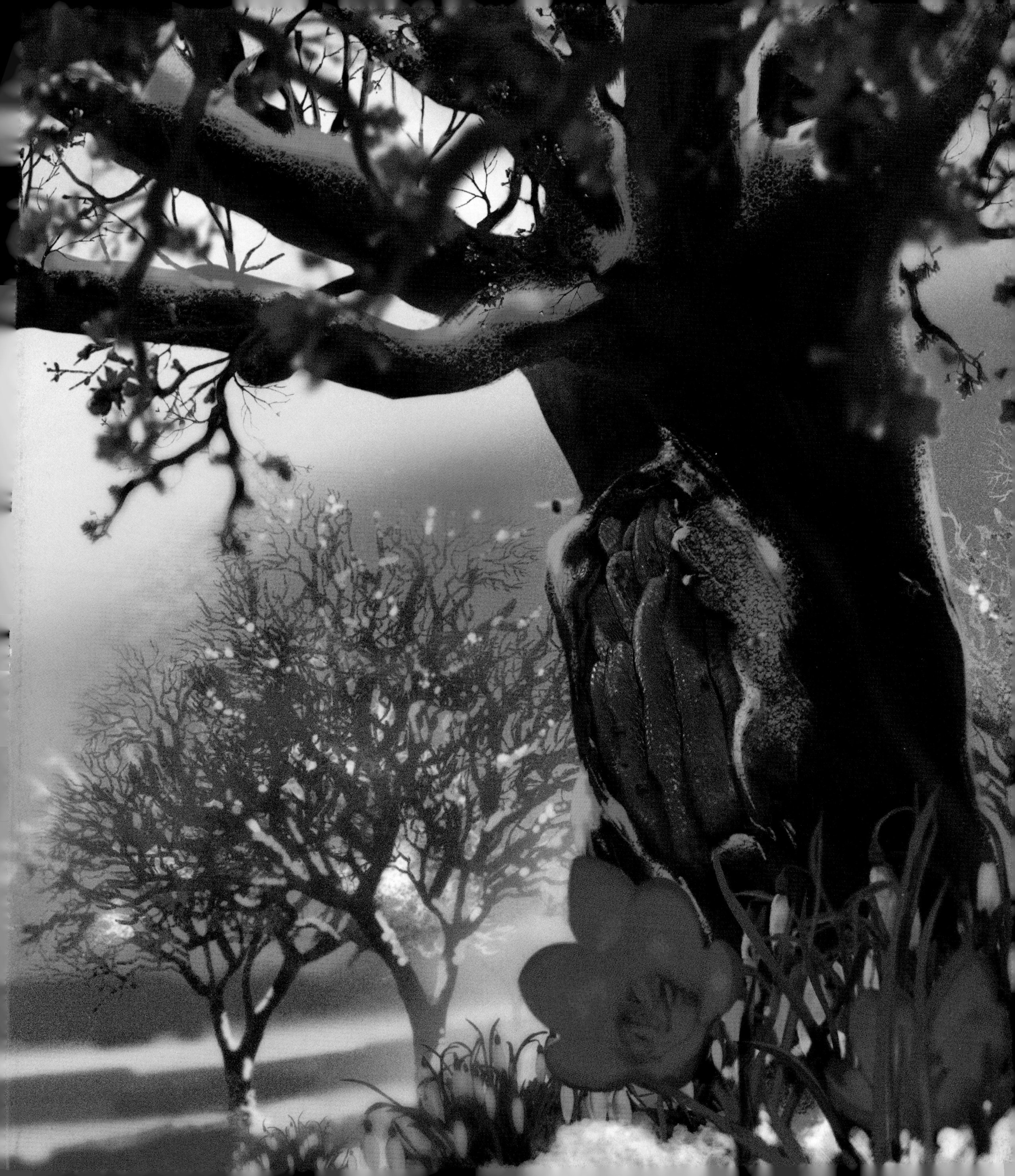

INSIGHT KIDS
An Earth Aware Book

PO Box 3088
San Rafael, CA 94912
www.insighteditions.com

www.MANDALAEARTHEDITIONS.com

FOR WEB EXCLUSIVE CONTENT!

f www.facebook.com/InsightEditions
t @insighteditions

First published in the United States in 2013 by Insight Editions
Copyright © 2012 Weldon Owen Pty Ltd
Originally published in Great Britain in 2012 by Weldon Owen Pty Ltd

Text by Lynette Evans
Illustrations by Francesca D'Ottavi/Wilkinson Studios

Library of Congress Cataloging-in-Publication Data available.

ISBN: 978-1-60887-198-8

ROOTS of PEACE   Replanted Paper

Insight Editions, in association with Roots of Peace, will plant two
trees for each tree used in the manufacturing of this book. Roots of
Peace is an internationally renowned humanitarian organization
dedicated to eradicating land mines worldwide and converting
war-torn lands into productive farms and wildlife habitats. Roots of
Peace will plant two million fruit and nut trees in Afghanistan and
provide farmers there with the skills and support necessary for
sustainable land use.

Manufactured in China

10   9   8   7   6   5   4   3   2   1